Welcome to ALADD

If you are looking for fast, fun-to-read stories with colorful characters, lots of kid-friendly humor, easy-to-follow action, entertaining story lines, and lively illustrations, then **ALADDIN QUIX** is for you!

But wait, there's more!

If you're also looking for stories with tables of contents; word lists; about-the-book questions; 64, 80, or 96 pages; short chapters; short paragraphs; and large fonts, then **ALADDIN QUIX** is *definitely* for you!

ALADDIN QUIX: The next step between ready to reads and longer, more challenging chapter books, for readers five to eight years old.

Mini Mermaid Tales

Read more ALADDIN QUIX books!

By Stephanie Calmenson

Our Principal Is a Frog!
Our Principal Is a Wolf!
Our Principal's in His Underwear!
Our Principal Breaks a Spell!
Our Principal's Wacky Wishes!

Royal Sweets
By Helen Perelman

Book 1: *A Royal Rescue*
Book 2: *Sugar Secrets*
Book 3: *Stolen Jewels*
Book 4: *The Marshmallow Ghost*
Book 5: *Chocolate Challenge*

A Miss Mallard Mystery
By Robert Quackenbush

Dig to Disaster
Texas Trail to Calamity
Express Train to Trouble
Stairway to Doom
Bicycle to Treachery
Gondola to Danger
Surfboard to Peril
Taxi to Intrigue

Little Goddess Girls
By Joan Holub and Suzanne Williams

Book 1: *Athena & the Magic Land*
Book 2: *Persephone & the Giant Flowers*
Book 3: *Aphrodite & the Gold Apple*
Book 4: *Artemis & the Awesome Animals*
Book 5: *Athena & the Island Enchantress*
Book 6: *Persephone & the Evil King*
Book 7: *Aphrodite & the Magical Box*
Book 8: *Artemis & the Wishing Kitten*

Mini Mermaid Tales

by **Debbie Dadey**

Illustrated by
Fuuji Takashi

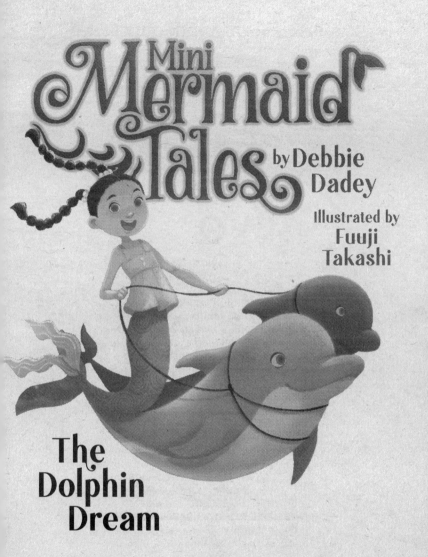

The Dolphin Dream

ALADDIN QUIX

New York   London   Toronto   Sydney   New Delhi

ALADDIN QUIX

Simon & Schuster Children's Publishing Division

1230 Avenue of the Americas, New York, New York 10020

First Aladdin QUIX paperback edition February 2024

Text copyright © 2024 by Debbie Dadey

Illustrations copyright © 2024 by Fuuji Takashi

Also available in an Aladdin QUIX hardcover edition.

All rights reserved, including the right of reproduction in whole or in part in any form.

ALADDIN and the related marks and colophon are trademarks of Simon & Schuster, LLC

Simon & Schuster: Celebrating 100 Years of Publishing in 2024

For information about special discounts for bulk purchases, please contact Simon & Schuster Special Sales at 1-866-506-1949 or business@simonandschuster.com.

The Simon & Schuster Speakers Bureau can bring authors to your live event. For more information or to book an event contact the Simon & Schuster Speakers Bureau at 1-866-248-3049 or visit our website at www.simonspeakers.com.

Cover designed by Karin Paprocki

Interior designed by Mike Rosamilia

The illustrations for this book were rendered digitally.

The text of this book was set in Archer Medium.

Manufactured in the United States of America 1223 OFF

2 4 6 8 10 9 7 5 3 1

Library of Congress Control Number 2023947595

ISBN 9781534489349 (hc)

ISBN 9781534489332 (pbk)

ISBN 9781534489356 (ebook)

To Alex

Cast of Characters

Aqua Wave: Mergirl

Shira: Aqua's older sister

Kiki: Friend of Shira's who rides dolphins

Rosie: Mergirl, new friend of Aqua's

Poppy: Friend of Rosie and Aqua

Freddie: Friend of Rosie and Aqua

Nanny Manny: Nanny who talks care of Rosie

Eduardo: Dolphin friend of Kiki's

Leslie: Dolphin friend of Kiki's

Shelly: Friend of Kiki's

Aunt Bella: Poppy's aunt

Mrs. Fast-Tail: Freddie's mother and owner of the newspaper

Mayor Ridge: Mayor of Trident City

Contents

Meet Aqua

Creatures swam by **Aqua Wave**'s house every day. Once she saw a nurse shark. Another time she saw a giant octopus!

But today she saw her most

favorite creature of all: a dolphin.
Aqua *loved* dolphins. She knew
a lot about them. But most of all,
she really wanted to ride one.
Aqua moved slowly. She didn't
want to scare the dolphin away.

She swam closer and asked, "Can I ride . . . ?"

Wham! A big sunfish swam into her. Aqua fell back into a group of sea mice.

She popped away from the mice. She liked their glowing hairs, but not their sharp points. They hurt. **"Ouch."**

The sunfish glared at Aqua and swam away. The sea mice frowned and moved off too.

"Oh no," Aqua cried. Now the dolphin was gone. The sunfish

had **ruined** everything. Aqua had missed her chance to ride a dolphin. She closed her eyes and used her **imagination**.

She was soaring. She leaped out of the water on the back of a dolphin. *Wheeeeeeeee* . . . Her heart pounded in excitement. Could such a dream come true?

Dolphins can swim really fast. Not as fast as a black marlin, but faster than most sharks. Aqua was quick for a young mermaid, but not as speedy as those sea creatures. What would it be like to go so fast?

"What are you doing?" Her older sister, **Shira**, swam into their backyard.

"I'm thinking about riding a dolphin," Aqua said.

"No wavy way," Shira told her. "You might get hurt."

"Dolphins are gentle," Aqua said. She didn't like it when Shira told her not to do something. It made her want to do it more.

Shira shook her head. "They are

wild. I don't want you anywhere near one."

Aqua had heard lots of stories of mermaids riding dolphins. They were safe. In fact, the next day lots of merkids would be riding on dolphins in their city's Dolphin Dash. How fun would that be?

"But you know how much I love them," she told her sister. It was true. Aqua's bedroom was filled with dolphin pictures and posters. She even had a full-sized stuffed dolphin she had made from kelp.

"No buts," Shira said. "I'm supposed to take you to MerPark."

Aqua clapped her hands. Her merfriends would be at the park. Maybe they would also want to ride a dolphin. They could have dolphin races just like in the Dolphin Dash. That would be super amazing.

"Don't you have school?" Aqua asked. Shira went to Trident Academy, but Aqua had one more year before she could start there. Now she went to Mini Mermaids and Merboys. It was a school just for seven-year-olds, and Aqua went three days a week. She had made many merfriends and they all had fun together. She'd even learned more dolphin facts. Her teacher said dolphins have two stomachs!

"Not today," Shira said. "Maybe some of my merfriends will be at the park."

Aqua grinned. If she was lucky

enough to see another dolphin, Shira would be too busy to keep an eye on her.

"Let's go!" Aqua raced toward the park.

2

Super Star

Aqua squealed when she saw her friends among the other merpeople at MerPark. "I'll meet you later at the slide," she told her sister.

"Stay where I can see you. I'll be over there with **Kiki**." Shira

pointed to a mergirl with a pretty purple tail. Aqua wished she had a purple tail like Kiki, or even a red tail like Shira's. Aqua's wasn't green and it wasn't blue. It was a

mix. No one had a tail like hers.

Luckily, her merfriends had tails that looked different too. **Rosie** was a friend she'd made before starting Mini Mermaids and

Merboys school. Her tail was red with zigzags. **Poppy**'s was bright yellow with swirls, and **Freddie**'s tail had green-and-orange stripes.

"I have a super idea," Rosie said when Aqua swam up to her mer-friends. "Let's play school. We can pretend to be in art class and paint shells."

Aqua groaned. Rosie *always* wanted to play school. Aqua liked it too, especially when she got to be the teacher, but not all the time.

"I have a super star idea too,"

Poppy said loudly, spinning around. "Let's make up a song and dance to it."

Freddie shrugged. "I don't know. What else can we do?"

Aqua blurted out, "Let's find some dolphins and ask to ride them!"

Poppy, Rosie, and Freddie gasped. **"Aqua!"** Freddie said. "That might be fun, but it doesn't sound safe."

Rosie patted Aqua's hand. "It could be **dangerous**."

Oh no. Her friends sounded just like her sister. "Dolphins aren't dangerous," Aqua told them.

Freddie **shivered**. "Dolphins swim really fast."

Aqua grinned. "I know. That's what will make it fun."

Freddie's face turned green. It almost matched his stripes.

"Dancing and singing are much safer," Poppy added.

"Let's sing and dance first," Rosie said. "Then we can play school."

"But what about the dolphins? Don't you want to look for them?" Aqua asked.

Freddie waved his hands in the water. "It doesn't matter. There aren't any dolphins around here." He looked happy about that.

Aqua wasn't happy. Seeing a dolphin that morning had made her want to see another. And to ride one.

"Sorry, I have to stay where **Nanny Manny** can see me," Rosie said. "I don't want to get in more trouble." They looked over to where Nanny Manny sat on a bench, not far from Shira and Kiki.

"Why are you in trouble?" Poppy asked.

Rosie shrugged her shoulders. "I used the back of my uncle's papers to draw pictures. I didn't know they were **important**." Rosie's uncle was the mayor of Trident City.

"Let's just sing and dance. Then we'll play school," Freddie said.

"If we can't search for dolphins,

then forget about school and everything else," Aqua snapped. She was in a bad mood.

Rosie waved a finger at Aqua. "Don't be **rude**."

Aqua wanted to go home. Now. She wasn't sure she even wanted to be friends with these merkids.

"I can't play anymore. Shira and I have to go home." Aqua swam away.

3

Dolphin School

"Aqua, stop!" Freddie called to her. "Please!"

Aqua didn't want to stop. She wanted to go home. Why couldn't they do what *she* wanted this time? But she turned around anyway.

"Why don't we have a lesson on dolphins?" Freddie asked. "You can be the teacher."

"Thanks!" Aqua smiled. "I can teach you everything I know about them."

Aqua's friends sat down on some rock seats. "Now, class," Aqua said in her best teacher voice. "Did you know that dolphins are very smart mammals?"

"Can they do math?" Rosie raised her hand. "I am very good at math now."

Aqua shook her head.

"Can they read books?" Freddie asked.

Aqua frowned.

"I like to read, but I like danc-ing more," Poppy said. "Do you

think dolphins can dance?"

Aqua nodded. "Well, the spinner dolphin spins like it's dancing."

First, Poppy jumped up and spun around.

Then, Rosie joined in and

danced and twirled on her red tail.

And lastly, Freddie hopped up and spun too!

This wasn't what Aqua wanted. "Class, sit down!" she snapped.

"Do we have to?" Poppy said. "We're just acting like dolphins."

Aqua twisted her tail fins. Being a teacher wasn't easy. "Please sit down. Let's get back to our lesson.

"Dolphins have very good vision. And do you know that they use clicks to sense things around them?"

"What's a click?" Freddie asked.

"That's a good question. A click is a noise that sounds like a creaking door or a loud buzz," Aqua answered. "Each dolphin also has their own special **whistle**."

"I can whistle," Freddie blew out a shrill sound that hurt Aqua's ears.

"Wow!" Rosie cheered. "Let me try."

Rosie only blew bubbles, but Poppy did a soft whistle. Freddie's whistle was very loud and sounded like a broken horn. All the noise was giving Aqua a **headache** and she covered her ears.

"Class, please be quiet. Dolphins do whistle, but I'm not sure how they sound. I don't know how to do it."

"I do," said a **surprise** voice, floating up beside them.

4

Whistles and Clicks

It was a friend of Shira's! "Hi," she told Aqua, Rosie, Freddie, and Poppy. "I'm **Kiki**. I live at Trident Academy."

"You live in a school?" Rosie

asked. "That is super. You must be very, very smart."

Kiki laughed. "I live there because my home is far away. I heard you talking about dolphin whistles."

"I can't do it," Rosie said sadly.

"It takes a while to learn," Kiki told them. "First, pucker your lips." Aqua giggled when her merfriends stuck out their lips.

"Now, curl your tongue," Kiki said. "Then blow."

Freddie's whistle was even

louder than before, but it did sound better. Poppy and Aqua made tiny toots. Even Rosie made a little sound. "I did it," she shouted. "Just like a dolphin."

"Do you know how to make dolphin clicks?" Freddie asked.

Kiki nodded. "My mom and dad can speak to many animals. They taught me."

"Oooh," Aqua shouted. "Teach us, please."

Shira swam over to join them. "Come on, Kiki. You don't have to play with these small fry."

Aqua frowned. She didn't like it when her sister called her small, even though Aqua was tiny compared to her merfriends.

"It's fun talking like a dolphin," Kiki told them. "First, try this squeak. *Squuuueak.*"

Together they made the sound. Rosie's was more like a screech than a squeak. "Pretty good," Kiki told them. "Try it again."

"What does that mean?" Poppy asked.

"It means 'hello' in Dolphin,"
Kiki said. "Now let's try a click.
Just curl your tongue on the top
of your mouth and flick it."

CLICK! CLICK! CLICK!

"I did it," Poppy cheered. Everyone was whistling, clicking, and

squeaking. Aqua's head wasn't hurting anymore, even though it was noisy. It was good noise.

"This is great," Rosie told them.

Aqua nodded. It was the most fun she'd ever had playing school. "We sound like a pod of dolphins." She still wished to ride a dolphin, though. It was too bad there weren't any around.

Then she looked behind her and was very, very surprised.

Dolphins

Not one. Not two. Not three, but four **bottlenose** dolphins had appeared!

"*Squeak,*" one said with a grin.

"*Squeak.*" Aqua said hello to a dolphin.

Kiki splashed her purple tail

before making lots of clicking and squeaking sounds. Two of the dolphins answered her.

"What are you saying?" Freddie asked.

Kiki waved to the dolphins. "I'd like you to meet **Eduardo**, **Leslie**, and their children. They are friends of mine. They heard us speaking in Dolphin."

"You are friends with dolphins?" Aqua couldn't believe it. Kiki was amazing.

"Five of my brothers saved

them from a fishing net and we've been friends ever since," Kiki explained.

"You have five brothers?" Poppy said. "I have one and he bothers me all the time."

Kiki laughed. "I actually have seventeen brothers."

"Wow!" Freddie cheered. "That sounds cool."

"Do you know what else is cool?" Kiki said. "Eduardo and

Leslie want us to swim with them around the park. They want to practice for the Dolphin Dash."

"Yes!" Aqua loved the Dolphin Dash. It was a race that happened every year in their city.

But at the same time Shira and Freddie shouted, **"No!"**

Freddie shrugged. "I don't want to go fast."

"But your last name is Fast-Tail," Rosie said. Freddie stared at the sand without looking up.

"Freddie can do what he wants," Aqua said. She didn't want him to feel bad. "I really, really want to swim with Eduardo and Leslie."

Shira shook her head. "No wavy way. It's not safe. We are going home now."

"Please, Shira," Aqua begged. "Please."

Shira frowned. "I don't want you to get hurt."

"My brothers and I swim with them all the time," Kiki said. "My friend **Shelly** and I are riding Eduardo and Leslie tomorrow in the Dolphin Dash."

"How exciting!" Aqua crossed her fins. Surely Shira would let her swim with Kiki's friends.

"No," Shira said.

Aqua felt like crying. She finally had the chance to swim with dolphins, and her mean sister wouldn't let her.

"Eduardo and Leslie are very gentle," Kiki said softly.

"Please, please, please, please,"
Aqua begged.

Shira tapped her chin with her
tail and answered. . . .

6

Wheeee

"No." Shira grabbed Aqua's arm and pulled. "Let's go."

"But why?"

Shira's face turned bright red, almost as red as her tail. "If you

must know, I fell off a dolphin
once and hurt my tail."

Aqua was surprised. "I'm sorry,
but I'm just swimming, not riding."

"It's a bad idea," Shira said. "I'm afraid for you."

"I'll be very careful. I promise," Aqua told her sister.

Shira looked at Kiki and took a deep breath. "All right," she said. "But only because Kiki says it's okay. I trust her."

Aqua hugged her sister. She hugged Kiki. She wanted to hug everyone. She turned to the dolphins and said, "Thank you so much. I've always wanted to swim with dolphins."

The dolphins stared at her. Aqua looked at Kiki. "How do I say 'thank you' in Dolphin?"

Kiki made a click, followed by a squeak. Aqua tried it, but the dolphins shook their heads and laughed. "Did I get it wrong?" she asked Kiki.

Kiki smiled. "You told them their ears were snotty."

"Oh no. Let me try it again." Aqua slowly made the thank-you sound, and Leslie smiled.

"I'm a little scared," Rosie whispered.

"You don't have to go," Aqua told her. "You can watch with Shira."

"I want to do it." Rosie nodded.

"Me too!" Poppy shouted.

With a splash, the dolphins were off. Aqua followed. To her surprise everyone came along, even Freddie and Shira. "I have to make sure you are safe," Shira told her.

Rosie cheered as they swam in a circle around MerPark.

"Dolphins are so pretty," Poppy said.

Aqua nodded. The dolphin family glided through the water like magic. They went slow for

dolphins, but fast for merkids.

Suddenly, the dolphins stopped. Leslie, Eduardo, and their children clicked and squeaked. "What's wrong?" Aqua asked

Kiki. Couldn't they swim more?

"Are they saying goodbye?" Freddie asked.

Kiki shook her head. "Actually, Shelly is here and it's time to practice for tomorrow's big race."

A mergirl with red hair hopped on Leslie's back. Kiki slid onto Eduardo and waved. With a swish, they zoomed away. "Wow! Look at them go," Poppy yelled.

"I'm going to cheer for them at the race tomorrow. I hope they win," Freddie said.

Aqua nodded. How exciting to have met four dolphins, and to know two mergirls who were riding in the Dolphin Dash. The only thing more exciting would be to ride a dolphin herself!

Dolphin Dash

"This is so fun!" Aqua told her sister the next day.

The Dolphin Dash was starting soon, and eight dolphins were lined up in the park. There would be three races, starting with young merkids about Aqua's age. Later would be teen riders, and this afternoon would be the adults. Aqua wanted to watch them all.

Shira held Aqua's hand. "Stay close, I don't want you to get lost in the crowd."

"I love the Dolphin Dash," Poppy said, coming up beside the two sisters. Poppy held her little brother on one hip. Their aunt **Bella** floated beside them.

"I'm so excited," Rosie said as she arrived with Nanny Manny. "This will be my first time seeing it."

Aqua smiled at them before waving to Freddie. He was on the other side of the dolphins with his mother, who owned the newspaper. **Mrs. Fast-Tail** was writing on a kelp notepad. The Dolphin Dash would be in tomorrow's newspaper for sure.

"Hi," Kiki said, floating up beside Shira.

"What are you doing here?" Shira asked. "Aren't you racing?"

Kiki shook her head. "My partner, Shelly, is sick with penguin pox and can't ride."

"Can't you find someone else?" Poppy asked. All dolphin teams had to ride in pairs.

Kiki shook her head. "I have let Eduardo and Leslie down. They came a long way to race." Eduardo and Leslie were in the crowd behind her, only a few merpeople away. They looked sad, but their children looked even sadder. Had they wanted to see their parents race?

"Maybe I could . . ." Aqua said.

"No!" Shira snapped.

Aqua nodded. Shira would never let her race. "I understand. You are afraid I will fall off like you did."

"Have you ever fallen off?" Rosie asked Kiki.

Kiki shook her head. "No, but it could happen."

"I could fly, but probably not," Poppy said. "Sometimes we worry about things that will never happen."

"But they could," Shira said.

"But they might not," Aqua whispered.

Mayor Ridge swam beside the dolphins with the start flag. Everyone huddled closer to the starting line to watch.

"Oh, please say yes, Shira. I will be as careful as can be. And Kiki will be with me." Aqua crossed her tail fins tightly and looked at her sister.

"**You can do it!** You can race!" Shira blurted.

Kiki squealed.

Rosie and Poppy clapped their hands.

Aqua hugged Shira. "You are the best sister ever."

Shira shook her head. "I just hope I'm doing the right thing. Be careful."

"We'll cheer for you!" Poppy squealed.

"Let's hurry." Kiki pulled Aqua toward Eduardo and Leslie.

Faster than a sailfish, Kiki and Aqua were on Eduardo and Leslie's backs. When Mayor Ridge

waved the flag, the race began!

"Wheeeeeeee," Aqua yelled as she clung tightly to Leslie's back. Kiki rode Eduardo. Freddie, Poppy,

Rosie, and Shira waved as the dolphins sped off around the park.

They went very fast. Maybe not too speedy for a dolphin, but it was super fun for a mergirl. The merpeople watching became a blur!

"Can we go faster?" Aqua called. The rules were that each team must ride side by side.

Kiki shook her head. "No, it's your first time and this is fast enough."

"You're right," Aqua said. "This is so cool!" Several dolphins were ahead of them, but a few were behind them as well.

"Hang on," Kiki said. "We're getting close to the finish line."

"Already?" Aqua could have kept going forever.

All around them, merpeople cheered for the team who won the race. Aqua was surprised that the cheering lasted as everyone finished. They even cheered for her!

Aqua hugged Kiki, Eduardo, and Leslie. "Thank you so much."

Leslie squeaked. "What did

she say?" Aqua asked Kiki.

"She said thank you for helping them be in the race. Their children really wanted to see them do the Dolphin Dash." Kiki and Aqua both smiled as their dolphin friends hugged their children.

"Are you **disappointed** that we didn't win?" Kiki asked her.

Aqua shook her head. "It was the most fun I've ever had."

Kiki squeaked to Eduardo and Leslie. They squeaked and bobbed their heads up and down.

Shira floated over to her and Aqua hugged her sister. "Thank you for letting me try something new. And thanks for letting my dolphin dream come true!"

Word List

bottlenose (BOT•ul•noz): A kind of friendly dolphin

dangerous (DAYN•jer•us): Might cause harm

disappointed (dis•uh•POYN•ted): Sad or displeased with someone or something

headache (HED•ake): Pain inside the head

imagination (IH•maj•a•NA•shun): Making a pretend picture in your mind

important (im•PORT•tunt): Worth a lot

rude (ROOD): Not polite

ruined (ROO•und): Messed up

shivered (SHIV•erd): Shook

surprise (sur•PRIZ): Not expected

whistle (WHIS•ul): A sound made by blowing air from the mouth

Questions

1. What animal is your favorite? Have you ever seen one in person?
2. Why didn't Shira want Aqua to ride a dolphin?
3. Is there more than one type of dolphin?
4. *Click* and *slick* are rhyming words. What's another word that rhymes with them?
5. What are two ways in which dolphins talk or communicate?

6. Do you know how to whistle?

If not, go to page 29 and try it!